Disney
Music Player
STORYBOOK®

Adapted by Tisha Hamilton

Adapted by Sarah Heller

CONTENTS

Reader's
Digest
Children's Books®

Pleasantville, New York • Montréal, Québec • Bath, United Kingdom

Play Song 1

"C'mon, Dad! It's time for school!" It was the day Nemo had been waiting for! Today he'd be going to school just like all the other kids. On the way there, Nemo peppered his father, Marlin, with questions. "Have you ever met a shark? How old are sea turtles?"

But Marlin was too nervous to listen. He was worried about his son. Nemo was the only survivor of a barracuda attack that had wiped out Marlin's entire family. And even so, Nemo was scarred by the experience—his egg had been damaged, and he was born with a little fin.

Marlin called it Nemo's lucky fin, but the truth was, it made Nemo an awkward swimmer. Marlin dreaded the time when he would no longer be able to keep his eye on Nemo.

Now that day had arrived. They swam to the school playground, where Nemo was introduced to the other kids and met his teacher, Mr. Ray. Marlin was reluctant to leave.

Nemo was embarrassed when he saw that his father was still in sight. "I'm okay, Dad!"

Marlin watched Nemo ride off with the others on Mr. Ray's back. Then he discovered where they'd gone. Mr. Ray was taking everyone to the Drop-off—where Nemo's family had been attacked! Marlin dashed off after them.

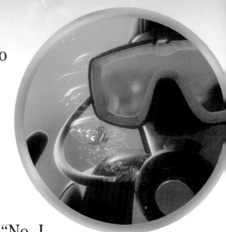

Play
Song
2
He found Nemo and his friends playing near a boat. Marlin confronted his son. "You were about to go into the Drop-off!" he scolded.

Nemo shouted back, "No, I wasn't!" He knew it wasn't safe to play that closely to a boat. Nemo had been nervous and he'd hung back.

"He was too afraid," agreed Nemo's friends.

Stung, Nemo wanted to show everyone he *wasn't* afraid. He swam right up to the boat and touched it with his fin. But he didn't see the diver that appeared behind him until it was too late. *Swish!* Nemo was caught in a net and scooped up by a human diver. Marlin watched the boat disappear. He had to get Nemo back!

Marlin swam back and forth, frantically. "Has anyone seen a boat?" he called.

A blue tang named Dory claimed to have seen the boat. She led him off. But she slowed down almost instantly. "I forget things," she explained.

Marlin and Dory were now face-to-face with some sharks who were trying to kick the habit of eating other fish. "Fish are friends—not food!" they chanted. As they ducked away from their toothy hosts, Marlin noticed a diver's mask. It belonged to the diver that took Nemo! It had writing on the strap: P. Sherman, 42 Wallaby Way, Sydney. Marlin and Dory were on their way!

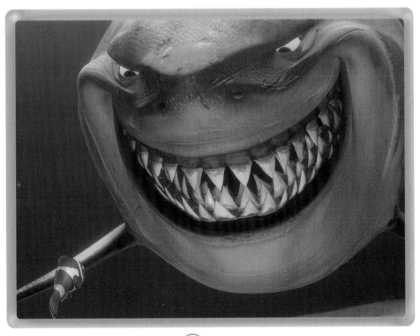

Play Song 3 Meanwhile, things couldn't have been more different for Nemo. A large hand dropped him into strange waters. Frantically, he swam this way and that. *Crash!* He kept bumping into something that wouldn't let him swim farther. He didn't know it yet, but he was in a fancy saltwater fish tank in a dentist's office.

Others were there, too—Bubbles, Peach, Deb, Gurgle, Jacques, Bloat, and Gill. When they found out that Nemo was an ocean fish and not from a pet store, everyone got excited. Only Gill, a black and white Moorish idol, knew anything about "the big blue."

Back in the ocean, Marlin and Dory asked a school of moonfish for directions to Sydney Harbor. But Dory did not remember the

Play
Song
4

special instructions
they gave her:
to swim through
the trench, not over it.
Before they knew it,
they were surrounded by
stinging jellyfish! Luckily, a
family of sea turtles that was riding
the swift East Australian Current rescued them.
As the group was carried along by the flowing
water, Dory and Marlin were able to rest up and
make friends. Marlin told a wide-eyed crowd of
turtle kids all about his search for Nemo. And
soon the story of the brave little clownfish on a
big mission made it all the way to Sydney Harbor.

That's where Nigel, the pelican who often visited the fish in Dr. Sherman's office, heard the story. He brought the news to Nemo and his friends. "He fought off sharks and a whole forest of stinging jellyfish looking for his boy, Nemo."

Nemo couldn't believe his ears. His dad who always worried was fighting sharks and jellyfish? The story made Nemo more desperate than ever to escape Dr. Sherman's office and find his dad! His days with the dentist were numbered anyway. Dr. Sherman planned to give Nemo to his scary-looking niece Darla as a birthday present.

Play Song 5 After saying good-bye to the friendly sea turtles, Marlin and Dory had just set off for Sydney when they got sucked into the gullet of a giant blue whale! Fortunately, the whale was also on his way to Sydney Harbor. Dory and Marlin found themselves at the top of a whale spout, with Sydney Harbor laid out below. They made it! But where to go from the harbor?

Before they had a chance to wonder, a pelican snapped the two fish up. But Marlin was so close to finding Nemo. He wasn't about to become a fish dinner, so he got himself stuck in the throat of the pelican. The bird spit them both out.

Play Song 6 They landed at the feet of Nigel, who recognized them. "Hop in my mouth if you want to find Nemo!" he told them. They flew off to Dr. Sherman's office.

They arrived just as Darla was holding her new fishy in its bag. And Nemo was doing the only thing he could think to do: he was playing dead. But Marlin didn't know Nemo was pretending. He was heartbroken!

Gill and the others took matters into their own fins. They helped Nemo get washed down the dentist's spit sink into the ocean. They knew Nemo would be able to meet up with Marlin there. Marlin very nearly swam away before he and Nemo were reunited.

But just as they found each other, something

terrible happened. Dory got netted by a fishing boat! Nemo knew he could help her. Would his father let him?

By now, Marlin knew just how brave and smart Nemo really was. He let his son swim inside the net and tell everyone to swim down. With Nemo's help, Dory and the others broke free of the net!

Weeks later, Nemo and Marlin were back home, safe and sound. School was a regular part of Nemo's routine, and Marlin was okay with that. Today, Nemo swam onto Mr. Ray's back with all the other kids, and Marlin watched them swim off without a twinge or a worry. But Nemo stopped them. "Wait!" he cried. "I forgot something." Nemo swam back to his father and gave him a hug. "Love ya, Dad!"

"I love you, too, son," said Marlin.

Disney THE
LION KING

Play Song 1

The sun rose on a new day in the Pride Lands. Mufasa, the Lion King, and his queen, Sarabi, were proud and excited. Today their newborn son, Simba, would be welcomed into the Circle of Life.

Mufasa and Sarabi took Simba to the top of Pride Rock. All the animals of the kingdom were gathered below to honor the newborn prince. The wise baboon, Rafiki, made a mark on Simba's forehead and then held the cub up high for all the animals to see. With screeches and roars of approval, the animals bowed their heads before the new prince.

As Simba got older, Mufasa taught his son many lessons about being the Lion King. "Everything the light touches is our kingdom," said Mufasa.

"What about that shadowy place?" The cub pointed to a dark smudge on the horizon.

"That is beyond our borders. You must never go there, Simba," was his father's answer.

Simba's jealous uncle, Scar, told him more. "It's an elephant graveyard. Only the bravest lions go there." Scar hoped the hyenas would kill Simba.

Simba had to see the graveyard for himself. Grabbing his friend Nala, they set off to explore together. But first they had to escape the watchful eye of Zazu, Mufasa's trusted advisor who was sent to chaperone them.

Play
Song
2

They got their chance at the watering hole. Slipping between the herds, the two little lions entered the dark, shadowy lands on their own. It was a scary place, filled with the old bones of long-dead elephants.

An angry Zazu caught up with them. He was busy scolding the cubs when they suddenly found themselves surrounded by a pack of hyenas.

"What have we got here?" asked one of the hyenas, eyeing Simba and Nala hungrily.

Simba gave a loud roar, but it was still too small to frighten off the hyenas. Luckily, Zazu rounded up Mufasa, who showed up just in time.

"Don't you ever come near my son again," Mufasa roared.

Play
Song
3
The hyenas backed away into the shadows at once, and Mufasa took the two cubs home to safety. No one realized that the hyenas had been sent by Scar.

Mufasa had a long talk with his son that night. "Look at the stars," he said. "The great kings of the past look down at us from the stars and they will always be there to guide you. And so will I."

Play Song 4

Scar was angry that his plan to kill Simba failed, but he wasn't giving up.

The next day, he told Simba to wait for him in the gorge. "I have a surprise that's to die for," Scar promised him.

Suddenly, a herd of wildebeests came pounding through the gorge. Terrified, Simba jumped onto a tree branch to escape the stampede. Then his paws began to slip. Mufasa arrived on the scene just in time, racing across the giant gorge to rescue his son. He scooped up Simba and dragged him off to safety. But now it was Mufasa who was in trouble. As the Lion King lost his balance and was caught up in the stampede, Scar watched from above.

Play
Song
5 Mufasa had very nearly climbed to
safety when one great swipe of his
brother's paw sent him tumbling to the
rocky canyon floor. And no one saw it.

"What have you done?" Scar turned on
Simba. "Run away and never return!" The older
lion smiled. Now he would become king.

Far from the Pride Lands, Simba made two
new friends who helped him forget his guilt
over the death of his father.
Pumbaa, the warthog,
and Timon, the meerkat,
taught Simba how to
forget the past, and to
live a worry-free life.

Simba grew to be
a strong young lion.

One day, a strange
lioness appeared
in their forest.

"Help, she's
going to eat me!"
wailed Pumbaa.
Simba faced the
lioness. With an expert

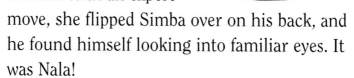

move, she flipped Simba over on his back, and
he found himself looking into familiar eyes. It
was Nala!

"You're alive," she said excitedly, "and that
means you're the king!" Nala explained to Simba
that Scar had turned the Pride Lands into a dusty
wasteland. "The herds left and now there is no
food," she told him. She begged Simba to come
back and challenge Scar.

Play Song 6

Simba was stunned. "I can't go back!" he cried. How could he explain to her that his father's death was all his fault? What would she think of him? He ran off into the night.

Mufasa's old friend Rafiki found Simba and reminded him of the night he and his father looked at the stars together. Looking up at the stars once more, Simba saw an image of Mufasa and heard his father's voice speak to him, "You are my son and the one true king." Simba knew what he had to do.

Back at Pride Rock, Simba faced Scar once more. "Step down, Scar," Simba growled. The older lion roared and lunged.

In the scuffle, Scar whispered in Simba's ear, "I killed Mufasa." Simba's eyes widened in shock. It wasn't his fault! And with one swift move, Simba sent Scar tumbling over the edge of Pride Rock—to the hungry hyenas below. With a mighty roar, Simba stood on Pride Rock and took his rightful place as the new Lion King.

Seasons passed and the rains returned. The Pride Lands were beautiful once again. Soon, it was time for Rafiki to present a new cub to the kingdom. This time, he held up the daughter of King Simba and Queen Nala for all to see.